Once there lived a little orphan boy who did not know either his real name or which country he came from. He did not know, because nobody knew. People at the children's home where he stayed called him Bobby.

Today Bobby was going to Disneyland with the other children. He sat all by himself on the bus. "I wish I belonged to a country—and that I knew which country it was," he thought. For Bobby didn't feel he belonged anywhere.

When the bus reached Disneyland, everyone went through the gates. Bobby became separated from the other children. For a while he looked around. Then in Fantasyland, he saw a beautiful palace with an enormous white and gold clock in front.

Bobby liked clocks. He had taken one apart once. But
this was the biggest clock he had ever seen. He got into
a boat for a closer look. As he sailed past the clock face,
he heard the chimes telling the hour.

Suddenly Bobby was in an enchanted land. The signs said "welcome" in many languages. A group of Scandinavian children sang to him, while ice skaters whirled about on a rink above the water.

A little farther on, the boat reached the British Isles. Wee folk were playing on a beautiful Irish harp. "Perhaps my real name is Patrick," said Bobby. "I do like green."

6

Then he heard English children singing to him from London Bridge and a little Scots Piper playing his bagpipes.

A flock of geese joined in the melody in Belgium, and in Holland boys and girls, seated on tulips, clicked their wooden shoes to keep time to the music.

When Bobby arrived in Spain and Portugal, the children there were playing and dancing.

"It's time we're aware,
 There's so much that we share," they sang.

When he reached Italy, future opera stars were singing
arias by the leaning tower of Pisa. Graceful dancers in
gay Paree were putting on a show. An Alpine yodeler's
voice rang out to the accompaniment of Swiss bells.

In Russia a row of Cossacks danced to a Balalaika Band.

The sky in the Middle East was filled with magic flying
carpets. What fun it would be to ride on one!

A little Greek shepherd boy played on his pipes of Pan.
"Why, they're all playing the same song!" thought Bobby.

There was a wonderful Indian snake-charmer.

A golden goddess reigned over the land of Bali.

Japanese boys were flying dragon kites above an orange
Tori gate.

And in Africa, what wonderful animals! Hippos, monkeys, giraffes, and a laughing hyena. Bobby liked animals. "Maybe I came from Africa," he said.

There was an Egyptian boy on his very own camel!

In South America everyone was dancing. Suddenly
Bobby wanted to dance with them.

He came to the end of the voyage with the words of the song running through his mind. "Just one moon, and a golden sun." And "A smile means friendship to everyone ...it's a small, small world."

He still did not know which country he came from, but he knew that a part of him belonged to every country. And a part of every country belonged to him!

The boat sailed out into the bright sunlight and
stopped. Bobby got out. He saw the boys and girls from
the children's home and ran to join them.

22

He felt alone no longer. He had friends all over the world! "It's A Small World"...after all!